Baxter Talks to God

by Sue Carlton Swinson
Ilustrated by Linda Shaw

J. McNeel Publications
Lubbock, Texas

Published by J. McNeel Publications
P.O. Box 93194
Lubbock, Texas, USA 79493-3194

Printed by Action Printing
Lubbock, Texas, USA 79423

Baxter Talks to God

by Sue Carlton Swinson
Illustrated by Linda Shaw

Find this yellow butterfly in the book.
A yellow butterfly brings happiness to everyone who sees it.

Dedication

To all the children who dream.

Chomp. Chomp. Chomp. Baxter Caterpillar sat on a limb munching a little green leaf. Baxter was looking across the garden at the beautifully colored flowers and insects. He was sad. Baxter wanted to be beautiful like the other insects.

Baxter saw a lady bumblebee buzzing from flower to flower. Her black and yellow colors were like soft velvet and her wings were sheer and shiny in the sunlight.

"She is so pretty," Baxter sighed, "and I am just a little, fat, brown worm.

Chomp. Chomp. Chomp. Baxter ate more leaves. He grew fatter. He grew sadder.

Two ladybugs were chatting on a nearby limb. Baxter looked their stunning colors. One ladybug was red and the other ladybug was orange. Both ladybugs had small, black dots on their tiny, delicate wings.

"They are brightly colored and I am just a little, fat, brown worm." Baxter said.

Chomp. Chomp. Chomp. Baxter ate more leaves. He grew fatter. He grew sadder.

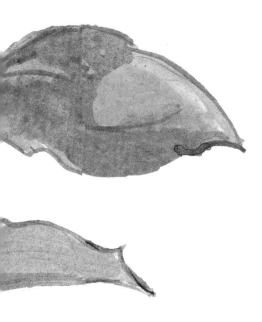

Baxter watched as a brilliant blue dragonfly soared above the green plants.

"Such a dazzling blue color and lovely silver wings," said Baxter.

Chomp. Chomp. Chomp. Baxter ate more leaves. He grew fatter. He grew sadder.

Baxter watched as a June bug lit on a vine of yellow flowers. The vine dipped in the breeze and came close to Baxter.

"What beautiful rainbow colors. In the sunlight he changes from blue to purple or green. The June bug is so dazzling he almost glows."

Chomp. Chomp. Chomp. Baxter ate more leaves. He grew fatter. He grew sadder.

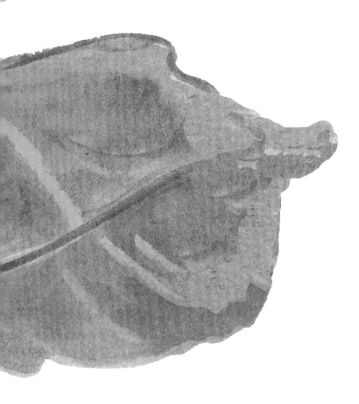

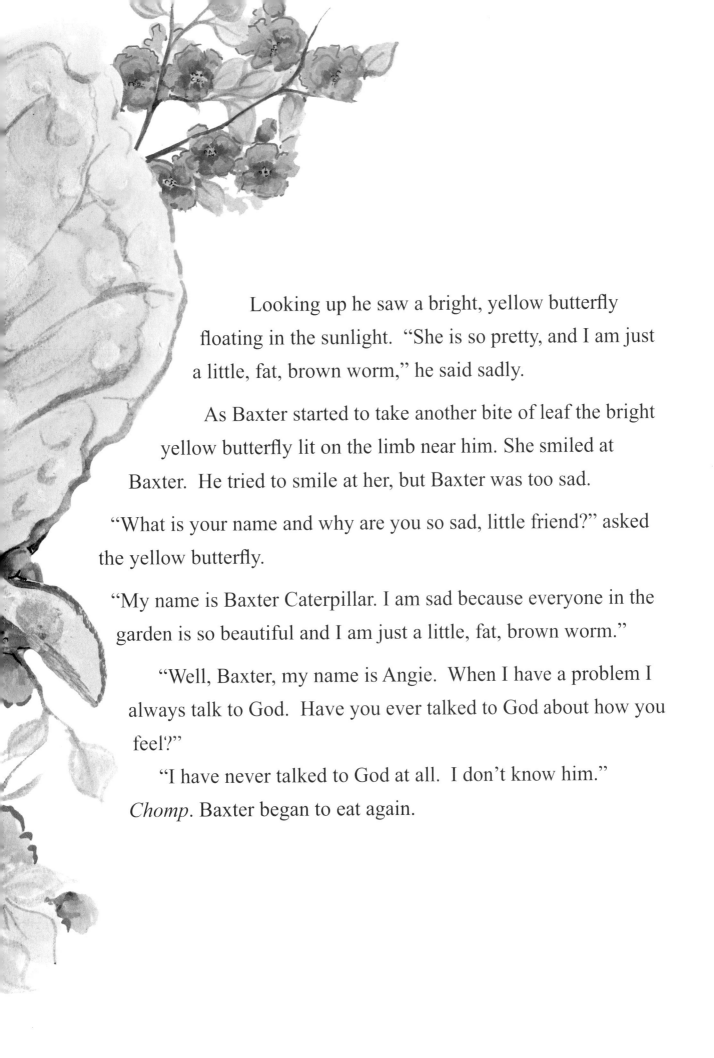

Looking up he saw a bright, yellow butterfly floating in the sunlight. "She is so pretty, and I am just a little, fat, brown worm," he said sadly.

As Baxter started to take another bite of leaf the bright yellow butterfly lit on the limb near him. She smiled at Baxter. He tried to smile at her, but Baxter was too sad.

"What is your name and why are you so sad, little friend?" asked the yellow butterfly.

"My name is Baxter Caterpillar. I am sad because everyone in the garden is so beautiful and I am just a little, fat, brown worm."

"Well, Baxter, my name is Angie. When I have a problem I always talk to God. Have you ever talked to God about how you feel?"

"I have never talked to God at all. I don't know him." *Chomp.* Baxter began to eat again.

"Baxter, you may not know God, but God knows you. He is the Awesome One who made us all."

"He is?" Baxter's eyes widened. "I wish God had made me a bright color like the other insects."

"Then you should talk to God and tell him how you feel. God will listen and he will answer your prayers."

"Prayers?" questioned Baxter.

"Baxter," Angie smiled, "when we talk to God it is called praying. Our talks with God are called prayers."

"Okay, I will talk to God. Where is he?" asked Baxter looking all around.

"God is everywhere. You can talk to him any time…any place. But you must believe in God to talk to him."

"I did not know about God until you told me about him, Angie. But now I believe in him.

How should I talk to him?"

"Like this, Baxter."

Angie folded her wings. "Close your eyes so you can only think about God. He will hear you."

Baxter folded his little caterpillar hands and closed his eyes.

"GOD!!!" he shouted. "IT'S ME, BAXTER."

"Baxter," Angie spoke softly, "you do not have to shout. God can hear the smallest whisper."

"Oh," Baxter whispered, beginning again, "God, it's me, Baxter. I am so glad to learn about you. Angie just told me."

"God knows, Baxter." Angie whispered.

"He does?" Baxter opened one eye and looked at Angie.

"Yes, God knows everything."

"Wow!" Baxter whispered.

"Just talk to God like he is your father," Angie said.

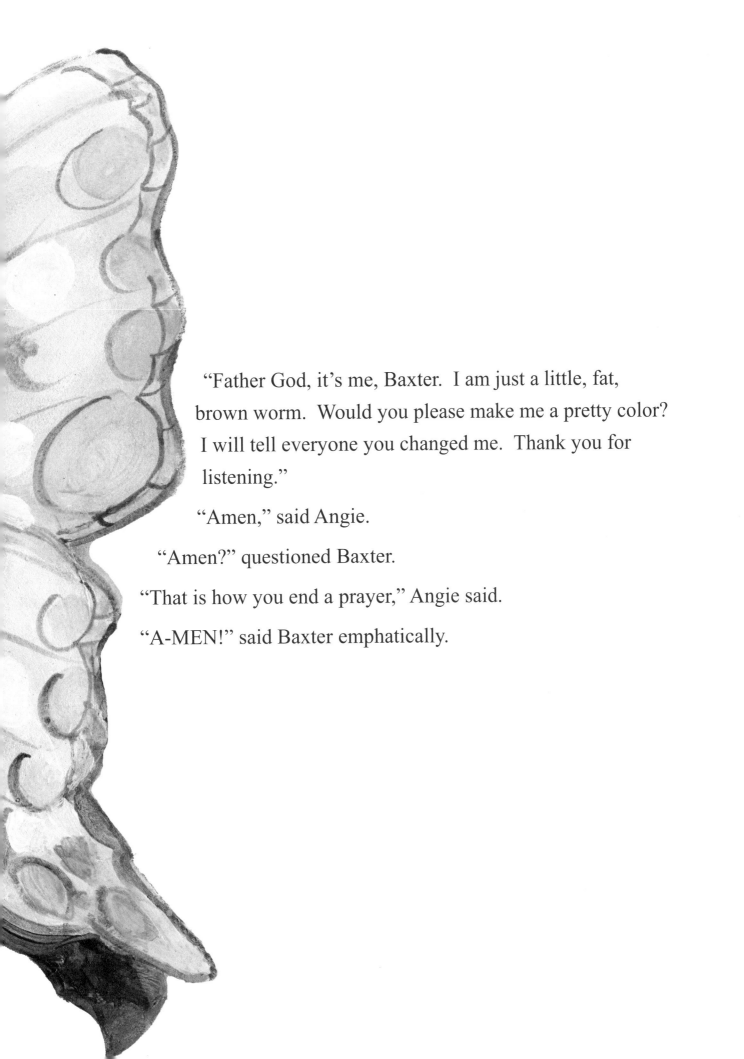

"Father God, it's me, Baxter. I am just a little, fat, brown worm. Would you please make me a pretty color? I will tell everyone you changed me. Thank you for listening."

"Amen," said Angie.

"Amen?" questioned Baxter.

"That is how you end a prayer," Angie said.

"A-MEN!" said Baxter emphatically.

Angie patted his little round head and said,
"Very good, Baxter."

"But, look at me," he said, "I'm not changed. I'm still a little, fat, brown worm. The prayer didn't work." Baxter looked sadly at his reflection in a dewdrop.

Angie smiled. "God will answer your prayers, Baxter. You will be changed very soon. Be patient and believe."

Baxter yawned very big. "All right, I will be patient and I will believe. I really will. But right now I am sleepy. I think I will wrap myself in my little blanket and take a nap while I wait."

"Good idea, Baxter," Angie said, as she flew away.

Baxter went to sleep wondering what color worm he would be when he awoke. Would he be red worm? Would he be blue worm? Would he have yellow strips or purple spots?

Baxter slept a very long time. He slept through the autumn.

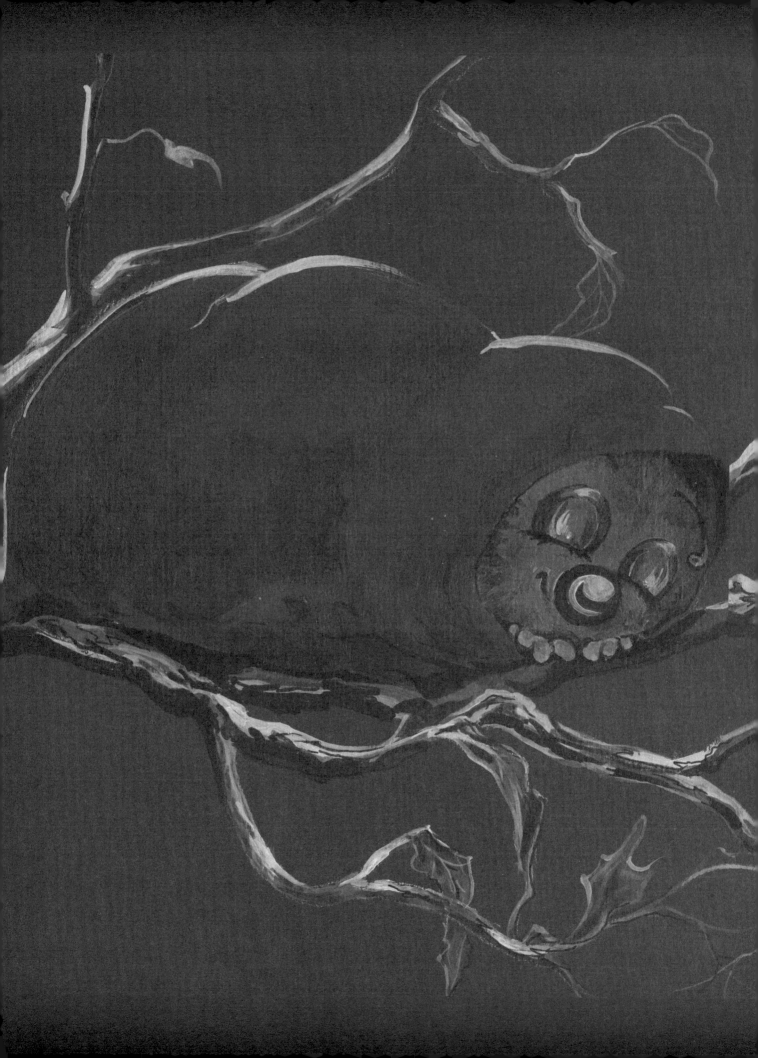

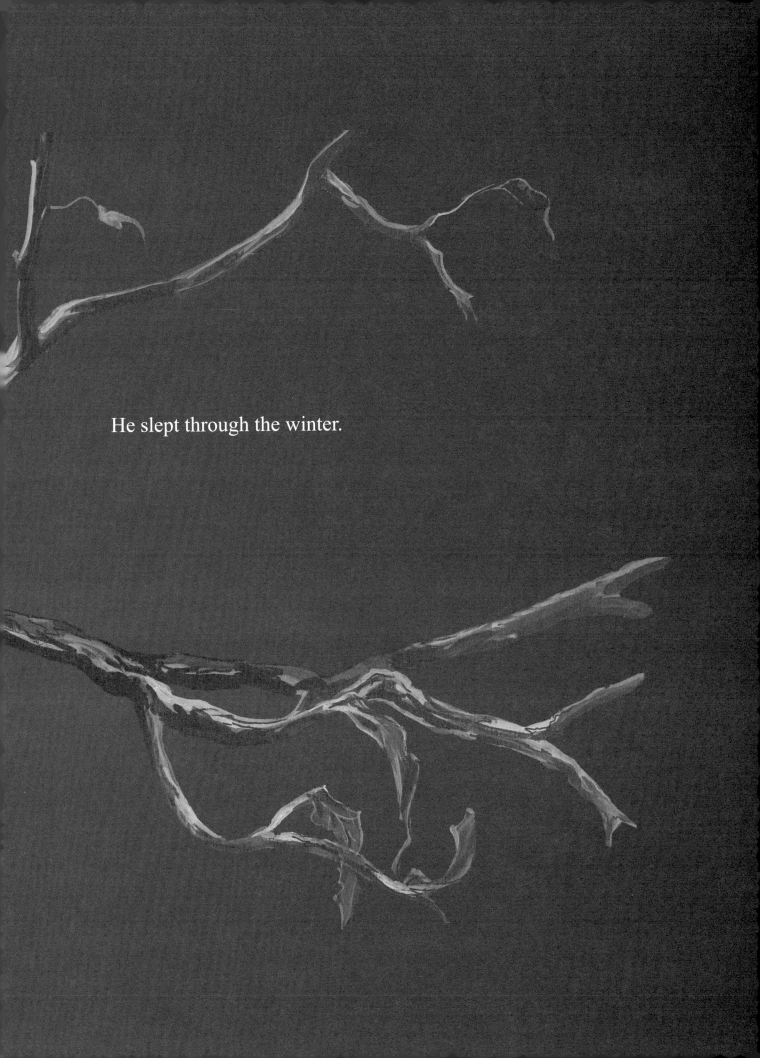

He slept through the winter.

One sunny day in spring Baxter
stirred, stretched, opened his eyes and
looked around. "That was a long nap,"
Baxter said, as he crawled out of his blanket
and sat on the limb. He blinked in the bright warm
sunlight. Baxter stretched again and as he did he grew
wider and wider. He felt very strange.

"What is different?" Baxter asked. "I do not feel like a
little, fat, brown worm. Maybe while I was sleeping
God answered my prayer. I wonder if I have changed
colors."

Baxter crawled over to look at his reflection in a raindrop puddle.

"WOW! WOW! WOW!" Baxter shouted. "I am gorgeous! I am absolutely GOR… GEEE…OUS!!! I am a beautiful, blue butterfly! Look at me! God changed me! He really did! He really did!" Baxter danced up and down the limb.

All the insects in the garden cheered.

Angie lit nearby.

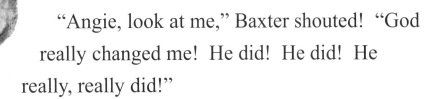

"Angie, look at me," Baxter shouted! "God really changed me! He did! He did! He really, really did!"

"Yes, he did, Baxter. You are now a handsome butterfly." Angie smiled. "God can change anyone."

Baxter closed his eyes and folded his 'gor- geee-ous' blue wings gently.

"Thank you, Father God. You changed me! You are awesome. You can change anyone. I will tell everyone about you. Thank you. Thank you. Amen."

"Amen," whispered Angie.

Then the two friends opened their beautiful wings and flew happily into the bright sunlight.

God really can change anyone.

About the Author...

Sue Carlton Swinson enjoys writing children's stories. She believes combining exciting stories and colorful illustrations will give hours of pleasure to the reader and listener. She wants her books to stir their imaginations and encourage children to read. Other books by this author are *The Butterfly Christmas* and *McMortie and the Tea Cakes.*

About the Illustrator...

Linda Shaw has had a lifetime career as an artist in various media. Her work appears across the country. In recent years she has illustrated a number of children's books. She finds it challenging and rewarding to transform the writer's vision into images which delight and stimulate the young reader.